May I Come In?

Written by Marsha Diane Arnold
Illustrated by Jennie Poh

Rain poured.

Raccoon shivered.

Thunder roared.

Raccoon quivered.

Lightning flashed.

Raccoon hid his head
under his arms.

"Being alone on a night
like tonight is scary."

Raccoon grabbed his umbrella
and hurried out the door.

Swish, plish.

Raccoon splashed through Thistle Hollow,
all the way to Possum's den.

"Possum, old friend, may I come in?"
Raccoon shouted over the thunder.

"What bad luck," Possum replied.
"My den's too small for one your size."

Swish, plish.

Raccoon splashed on through Thistle Hollow,
all the way to Quail's brambles.

"Quail, old friend, may I come in?"

"What bad luck," Quail replied.
"My brambles are tight. You're too wide."

Swish, plish.

Raccoon splashed on through Thistle Hollow,
all the way to Woodchuck's hole.

"Woodchuck, old friend, may I come in?"

"What bad luck," Woodchuck replied.
"I've only room for one to hide."

Raccoon stood shaking in the rain.

His umbrella blew inside out.

His fur felt wet and spongy.

He sniffled as he thought of
spending the night alone.

On the edge of Thistle Hollow, beyond the rain and darkness, he saw a tiny light, glimmering and shimmering.

Swish, plish.

Swish, plish.

Swish, swish, PLISH.

"Rabbit, old friend," called Raccoon doubtfully, "may I come in?"

Rabbit opened the door.

Behind her, ten little rabbits hopped
and bopped to the raindrops.

"Never mind, Rabbit," said Raccoon, backing away. "Your house is full."

"What good luck," said Rabbit.
"Come right in.
There's always room for a good friend."

Rabbit led Raccoon to a cozy chair.

Ten little rabbits hopped and bopped.

Rain poured.

Raccoon smiled.

Thunder roared.

Raccoon hummed.

Lightning flashed.

The smell of carrot stew filled Rabbit's home.

Soon a knock sounded over the thunder.

Three voices cried out from the rain and the darkness,

"Being alone on a night like tonight is scary."

Rabbit opened the door to . . .
Possum, Quail, and Woodchuck.

Ten little rabbits hopped and bopped.

Raccoon and Rabbit looked at
each other and grinned.

"What good luck," they said. "Come right in.
There's always room for *all* our friends."

Especially for my husband, Frederick Oak Arnold,
who always makes room for friends

—Marsha

For Jake, Aurelia, and Evangeline

—JP

Text Copyright © 2018 Marsha Diane Arnold
Illustration Copyright © 2018 Jennie Poh
Design Copyright © 2018 Sleeping Bear Press

Sleeping Bear Press®
2395 South Huron Parkway, Suite 200
Ann Arbor, MI 48104
www.sleepingbearpress.com

Printed and bound in the United States.

10 9 8 7 6 5 4 3 2 1

Library of Congress Cataloging-in-Publication Data

Names: Arnold, Marsha Diane, author. | Poh, Jennie, illustrator.
Title: May I come in? / written by Marsha Diane Arnold ; illustrated by Jennie Poh.
Description: Ann Arbor, MI : Sleeping Bear Press, [2018] | Summary: Raccoon
does not want to be alone on a stormy night but his neighbors, Possum,
Quail, and Woodchuck, each tell him they have no room to spare.
Identifiers: LCCN 2017029803 | ISBN 9781585363940
Subjects: | CYAC: Thunderstorms—Fiction. | Neighborliness—Fiction. |
Animals—Fiction.
Classification: LCC PZ7.A7363 May 2018 | DDC [E]—dc23
LC record available at https://lccn.loc.gov/2017029803